A New Home
for Truman

Look for all
the books in the

PET RESCUE CLUB
series

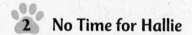

A New Home for Truman

by Catherine Hapka
illustrated by Dana Regan

studio BOOKS

White Plains, New York • Montréal, Québec • Bath, United Kingdom

cover illustration by Steve James

Published by Studio Fun International, Inc.
44 South Broadway, White Plains, NY 10601 U.S.A. and
Studio Fun International Limited,
The Ice House, 124-126 Walcot Street, Bath UK BA1 5BG
All rights reserved.
© 2015 Studio Fun International, Inc.
Studio Fun Books is a trademark of Studio Fun International, Inc.,
a subsidiary of The Reader's Digest Association, Inc.
Printed in China.
10 9 8 7 6 5 4 3 2 1
SL1/09/14

**The American Society for the Prevention of Cruelty to Animals (ASPCA®)
will receive a minimum guarantee from Studio Fun International, Inc. of $25,000
for the sale of ASPCA® products through December 2017.**

Comments? Questions? Call us at: 1-888-217-3346

Library of Congress Cataloging-in-Publication Data

Hapka, Cathy.

A new home for Truman / by Catherine Hapka

illustrated by Dana Regan.

pages cm -- (Pet Rescue Club; 1)

Summary: "When Janey starts a blog where people can share cute pet photos and
stories, she never imagines she'll receive a heartbreaking photo of a skinny, abandoned
dog. She calls on her friends Lolli, Zach, and Adam to help - and that's just the start!
When these animal-loving fourth graders discover how many animals need help in
their suburban hometown, they just can't sit by and do nothing."
Provided by publisher. Includes notes on how to get involved and a bookmark with
facts about the real rescue dog on which
the story is based.

ISBN 978-0-7944-3312-3 (paperback)

[1. Animal rescue--Fiction. 2. Dogs--Fiction. 3. Clubs--Fiction.]
I. Regan, Dana, illustrator. II. Title.

PZ7.H1996Neu 2015

[Fic]--dc23

2014024496

For all the shelter workers
who help people find their pets and pets find their people.

C.H.

1
The Best Birthday Ever!

"Happy birthday, Janey!" Lolli Simpson exclaimed.

Janey Whitfield set down her lunch tray at her usual spot across from Lolli. "It's not my birthday yet," she told her best friend with a smile. "Not until tomorrow, remember?"

"I know." Lolli pushed a lock of curly black hair out of her eyes. "But tomorrow is Saturday. I wanted you to be able to celebrate here at school with all your friends."

Lolli waved a hand at the other people sitting at the table. Their friend Adam Santos was next to Janey. Several kids from their fourth grade class were a little farther down, talking about that morning's spelling test.

"Come on, everybody!" Lolli called out. "Let's sing!"

She led the whole table in a round of "Happy Birthday to You." A few kids at nearby tables joined in. Janey loved every second of it. It was great having everyone sing to her!

"Thanks, everybody!" she called out when the song was finished. She waved, and some of the other kids waved back. Soon they all went back to their own conversations. "Thanks, Lolli," Janey told her friend. "That was fab." Janey loved to use interesting words whenever she could. Her favorite right then was "fab." It was short for fabulous.

"Wait—there's more." Lolli reached into her insulated lunch bag and pulled out a small reusable container. Lolli's parents liked to call themselves back-to-the-land hippies. They lived on a small farm outside of town and grew their own organic food. They bought most of their clothes at thrift stores and recycled everything. Lolli never brought brown paper bags or plastic baggies for her lunch like most of the other kids. She had a whole set of reusable bags and containers that she used instead.

"What is it?" Janey opened the container and peered at the grayish-brown lump inside.

"It's a cupcake." Lolli grinned. "Dad helped me make it just for you."

"Oh. Thanks." Janey smiled. "Um, it looks…interesting."

"That's a cupcake?" a new voice exclaimed loudly in Janey's ear.

Janey looked up. Zach Goldman had just stopped by their table. Zach was friends with Adam, but Janey didn't like him very much. He was rowdy, loud, and kind of obnoxious. Once when Janey had received the highest grade in the class on a math test, Zach had called her "Brainy Janey" for almost a month.

Zach leaned over for a better look at the cupcake. He was holding his skateboard under his arm, and the end of it poked Janey in the back.

"Ow," she said, pushing him away. "What are you doing?"

Zach grinned. "That doesn't look like a cupcake," he said. "It looks like something one of my mom's patients barfed up."

"Gross!" Janey made a face. Zach's mom

was a veterinarian. She treated most of the cats and dogs in town.

"It's a special recipe my dad made up," Lolli told Zach. "With zucchini, kale, and oatmeal. The cupcakes are actually really healthy, and totally organic, too."

"Zucchini and kale?" Zach said. "Do me a favor, Lolli. Don't make me a cupcake on my birthday."

With a grin, he hurried away.

Lolli looked worried. "Does it really look that bad?" she asked Janey. "I ate one of the cupcakes for breakfast, and I thought it was good."

Janey didn't like zucchini. But lots of the food at Lolli's house tasted better than it looked or sounded. So she forced herself to take a tiny bite of her birthday cupcake. She thought it would taste like mud, but it actually wasn't that bad.

"It's great," she said. "I love it. Thanks, Lolli, you're the best friend ever!"

Lolli looked relieved. "No, you are," she said. "So what are you going to do to celebrate your birthday tomorrow?"

That made Janey's smile get even bigger. "I can't wait until tomorrow," she said. "I'm pretty sure Mom and Dad are getting me something really special this year."

"Really? What?" Lolli was digging into her lunch bag again. While she wasn't looking, Janey nudged Adam. Then she broke off more than half of her cupcake and slipped it to him. She put a finger to her lips, and he nodded.

Adam popped the cupcake into his
mouth in one big bite. He chewed and
swallowed quickly. Then he gave Janey a
thumbs-up.

Janey smiled gratefully. Adam was pretty
skinny, but he ate a lot. And he liked almost
everything, including the cafeteria's baked
beans. Even Lolli's dog, Roscoe, wouldn't
touch those!

Thinking about Roscoe reminded Janey of her big news. She turned back to Lolli. "I think my parents are finally getting me a dog," she said.

Lolli's head snapped up in surprise. "Huh?" she said. "But your dad is so allergic to animals."

Janey's father's allergies were the reason Janey had never had a pet, even though she was crazy about animals of all shapes and sizes. Whenever Mr. Whitfield was around any creature with fur or feathers, he started wheezing and sneezing. His eyes turned red, and his nose turned redder. He sniffled nonstop. It even happened when he was around Janey's aunt's poodle. Janey had read that poodles weren't supposed to bother people with allergies as much since they didn't shed. But her parents had explained that it didn't really work that way.

"I know. But I figured out a way to compromise," Janey told Lolli. "See, I did some research on the Internet. I found out there are allergy shots for people with animal allergies! Isn't that great?"

"Allergy shots?" Lolli looked uncertain. "You want your dad to get shots so you can have a dog?"

"Uh huh. I printed out some articles about the allergy shots." Janey broke off a tiny piece of cupcake and ate it. "I started leaving them lying around the house about a month ago. I figured that would give Dad plenty of time to talk to his doctor about getting the shots. I also left some pictures and information about my favorite dog breeds."

"Really?" Adam looked up from his lunch. "What breeds did you pick?"

Adam was very interested in dogs. Even though he was only nine, he'd been running his own successful pet-sitting business for over a year. He fed and walked people's dogs for them after school and any other time they needed him. He also helped people train their dogs sometimes. He'd taught Roscoe how to shake hands and balance a dog treat on his nose.

"I was thinking about a Maltese or a papillon," Janey told him. "They both seem really cute and fun. And I thought maybe a small dog like that would mean Dad needs to get the shots less often."

Adam nodded. "I walked a Maltese once.

I liked her."

Lolli laughed. "You like every dog you walk, Adam," she said. Then she turned to Janey. "Maybe you don't need a fancy breed. What's wrong with a nice all-American mutt like Roscoe?"

"That would be fine, too. Roscoe is totally fab," Janey said. She meant it, too. Roscoe was a big, lovable goof who had come from the local animal shelter as a puppy. He was part rottweiler, part Labrador retriever, and part who-knew-what. Janey had spent many happy hours at Lolli's place playing fetch with Roscoe, swimming with him in the pond, or just lying in the grass rubbing his belly.

"I bet you could find a dog just as great as Roscoe at the Third Street Animal Shelter,"

Lolli said. "The dogs and cats there all really need homes. My parents and I go there sometimes to volunteer. Actually, Mom said we might go tomorrow to drop off some homemade dog and cat toys we made last weekend. I could help you look at dogs then if you want."

"That would be awesome," Janey said. "I'll mention it to my parents if they haven't gotten my dog yet. Come to think of it, they might be thinking the same thing. They donate money to the shelter every year." She sighed happily. "Anyway, I don't really care what kind of dog I get. I just can't wait to have one of my very own!"

She'd been dreaming about this day ever since she could remember. Janey had always loved animals—all animals. She read books about dogs, hung cute pictures of cats on her walls, and doodled horses and elephants and rabbits all over the margins of her school notebooks. She loved spending time with Roscoe, Adam's dog-sitting clients, and any other animal that came along. But nothing would compare to having a pet of her very own, to cuddle and snuggle with any time she wanted.

It was going to be so great! She shivered with excitement, wondering how she was ever going to wait until tomorrow.

2
Birthday Surprises

Janey woke up early the next morning. For a second she couldn't remember why she was excited. Then she smiled.

"Happy birthday to me!" she said, jumping out of bed.

She pulled on her bathrobe and raced downstairs. The smell of banana pancakes and bacon greeted her.

"Happy birthday, sweetheart!" Janey's father sang out. He was at the stove with a spatula. "I'm making your favorite breakfast."

"Thanks, Daddy." Janey looked around the kitchen. There was a pile of wrapped gifts on the counter. None of the packages had air holes that she could see.

But she couldn't see her mother, either. Maybe Mom was out in the garage with the dog, waiting to surprise her.

Then her mother hurried in from the living room. "Happy birthday, Janey, love!" she said. "How does it feel to be a year older?"

"Fab," Janey said. Her father set a platter of pancakes and bacon in front of her, and Janey helped herself. "I can't wait to see what you got me this year!"

Her parents traded a smile. "We can't wait, either," Janey's father said. "Eat your birthday breakfast, and then you can open your gifts."

Janey loved banana pancakes and bacon. But that morning, she hardly tasted them. She ate as fast as she could.

"Finished!" she said, gulping down some juice. "Time for presents."

Her parents both laughed. "All right," her mother said. "Go ahead, love."

Janey grabbed one of the gifts and shook it. Even if there wasn't a dog in the pile of gifts, maybe the packages contained dog stuff, like a collar and leash or food dishes or dog toys. Now that she thought about it, that made more sense anyway. Then Janey would be all ready to go and pick out her own dog at the shelter. She couldn't wait!

She ripped the paper off the first gift. "Oh," she said in surprise.

There was no collar or leash. No dishes or dog toys, either. Just a shirt with a sparkly collar.

"It's the one you liked at the mall last weekend, remember?" her mother said with a smile.

Janey nodded. She did like the shirt, even if she wasn't that excited about it right now. But maybe she could wear it to the shelter when she chose her dog.

"Thanks," she said. "Next!"

For a second she thought the next gift was a collar, but then she realized it was a bracelet. Janey opened several more packages after that, but all of them contained non-dog gifts.

Finally there was only one gift left. That had to be the dog gift!

Janey picked it up. "Don't shake that one, sweetheart," her father said.

Janey nodded. She had a bad feeling about this. The shape and weight of the gift didn't seem right for any kind of dog stuff. It was light and rectangular.

She opened it quickly. "Oh," she said. "A tablet computer."

"This model just came out last week." Her father sounded excited. "We knew you'd love it!"

Her mother nodded. "Your laptop is getting old," she explained. "This will be so much better."

"It's already fully loaded, too," her father said. "It's got a great browser, a kid-safe blogging platform, and of course all your favorite games—like Puppy Playtime."

Janey perked up. "Puppy Playtime?" she echoed with a smile. "Yes, I do love that game."

She paused, waiting for her parents to say something else about puppies—like that they were taking Janey to get one! But her father just went on talking about the other software on the tablet.

"What's wrong, love?" Janey's mother interrupted her husband. "You don't look as excited as we expected."

Janey bit her lip. Were her parents teasing her? That didn't seem like them.

"What about my dog?" she blurted out.

"Dog?" Janey's mother traded a look with Janey's father.

"Oh, Janey." Her father shook his head. "Is this about those printouts I found on my desk a couple of weeks ago?"

Janey nodded. "Did you read them? All you need to do is get a few shots and you won't be allergic to animals anymore!"

"I'm afraid it's not that simple," Janey's mother said. "We looked into the shots once, but the doctor advised against it because your father has mild asthma."

Janey couldn't believe that this was happening. She felt her face turning red. If she didn't get away, she'd start crying or yelling—probably both.

"I...I need to call Lolli," she choked out. "I think she wants me to come to her house."

Her mother looked worried. "Are you sure? We were going to watch a movie, or—"

Mr. Whitfield put a hand on his wife's arm. "It's okay, Janey," he said softly. "Go ahead and call Lolli. We can watch that movie later."

There was no answer on the phone at Lolli's farmhouse, so Janey called Lolli's mom's cell phone. It turned out that the whole family was in the car on their way to the shelter.

"We're just five minutes from your house," Mrs. Simpson told Janey. "We'll swing by and pick you up. I know you love visiting the animals at the shelter."

"Thanks," Janey said.

While her father cleared the break-fast dishes and her mother picked up the wrapping paper from her gifts, Janey ran upstairs to change out of her pajamas. Then she stood in the front hall until she saw the Simpsons' battered old station wagon pull to the curb in front of her house.

"Lolli's parents are here to pick me up," she called. "I'll be back in a while."

Ten minutes later, she was walking into the Third Street Animal Shelter with Lolli and her parents. Mr. Simpson was carrying a hemp bag filled with homemade dog and cat toys. Mrs. Simpson had a bag of organic kale from her garden. She'd explained that it was for some pet rabbits that had come into the shelter that week.

The shelter was a one-story brick building tucked between the post office and a florist shop. Inside, the lobby was painted with cheerful murals of cats, dogs, and other animals. The muffled sound of barking came from beyond a door marked Dog Room.

"I expected to come here today," Janey said sadly, staring at that door. "But I thought it would be to pick out my own dog."

Mrs. Simpson put her arm around Janey's shoulder. During the ride over, Janey had told Lolli and her parents what had happened.

A young woman came out from behind the front desk and hurried over. She was in her twenties, with a blond ponytail and a bright smile. "Oh, you brought the toys!" she exclaimed. "Thanks so much—I know the critters will love them."

"You're welcome, Kitty," Mrs. Simpson said.

That made Janey smile. "You work in an animal shelter, and your name is Kitty?" she asked the young woman.

Kitty laughed. "Actually, it's Kathleen," she said. "But after I smuggled a whole litter of kittens into my room as a kid, my family started calling me Kitty. And I guess it stuck!"

"It's Janey's birthday today," Mr. Simpson told Kitty. "Can she play with some animals to help her celebrate?"

"Of course!" Kitty said. "Go on into the Meet and Greet Room, and I'll bring somebody in for you to play with. Would you prefer cats or dogs?"

"I love both," Janey said. "But I especially like dogs, I guess."

She followed Lolli through a doorway across from the front desk. Inside was a small room with a tile floor. There were benches and beanbag chairs, as well as several scratching posts and a bucket filled with toys and treats.

Soon Kitty returned. She was leading two half-grown puppies. One was a small terrier mix, and the other was a tall, gangly brown dog whose fringed tail never stopped wagging.

"This is Buster, and this is Lyle," Kitty said. "They're both super friendly and playful. Go ahead and wear them out if you can— you'll be doing me a favor!" She laughed and left, pulling the door shut behind her.

"Oh, you're adorable!" Janey exclaimed, falling to her knees and cuddling the puppies. For a second she felt happy, like she always did when animals were around. But she felt sad at the same time. She would love to take home either Buster or Lyle—or better yet, both of them! But that wasn't going to happen.

"They're so cute!" Lolli exclaimed, giggling as Lyle licked her chin. "I bet Roscoe would love a couple of puppies to play with!"

"Don't even think about it," her mother said with a laugh. "One dog is more than enough for this family."

"Oh, well." Lolli smiled. "At least I can play with them here." She turned to Janey. "That gives me a great idea. Why don't we volunteer here at the shelter together? They let kids help out if their parents sign a form. We could come once or twice a week after school."

"That sounds fun," Janey agreed. "Not as much fun as having my own pet, but better than nothing." She hugged Buster as he wiggled onto her lap. "A puppy would be a lot cuddlier than some stupid old tablet."

"I know," Lolli agreed. "Your tablet sounds cool, though. Does it take pictures? Too bad you didn't bring it with you, or I could take some photos of you with Buster and Lyle."

"Yeah." Janey tickled Buster under his furry chin. "But wait—that gives me a totally fab idea…"

3

Janey's Big Idea

Half an hour later, the Simpsons dropped Janey and Lolli off at Janey's house. Janey rushed inside. "Mom! Daddy!" she yelled. "Where are you?"

Her mother came into the front hall from the kitchen. "Hello, Lolli," she said. "Janey, you look like you're in a better mood than when you left."

"I'm sorry about earlier," Janey said, hurrying over to give her mother a hug. "You too, Daddy," she added as her father wandered in carrying a news magazine. "I loved all my presents, even if none of them is a dog."

"Good, good." Her father looked relieved. "I'm sorry we can't get a pet, sweetheart."

"I know. But listen, I had a great idea that might be the next best thing," Janey said.

Her mother smiled. "Uh oh," she said. "What is it—a robot dog?"

Lolli giggled. "That definitely sounds like something Janey would invent!"

Janey giggled, too. "Maybe someday. But my great idea does involve technology— namely, my awesome new tablet!" The tablet was still on the table where she'd left it. She hurried over and picked it up. "You said this has a blogging program, right?"

"Yes," her father said. "It's a brand new platform made specifically for bloggers under fourteen. There are all kinds of safety features, and—"

"Perfect," Janey interrupted. "Because that's my idea. I'm going to start a blog! It'll be called, um, Janey's Pet Place, and kids can use it to share cute pictures of their cats and dogs and other pets."

"What a wonderful idea, love!" her mother said.

"I know." Janey smiled. "That way, it'll be like I have all the pets in town around me all the time!" She grabbed Lolli's hand. "Come on, I can't wait—let's go up to my room and figure out how to get started!"

An hour later, Janey was feeling both excited and frustrated. "The text we wrote is perfect," she told Lolli, "but it won't do any good if we can't figure out how to get the blog set up the way I want it!"

"I know, right?" Lolli poked at the tablet's onscreen keypad. "If this blog thingy is made for kids, shouldn't it be easy to use?"

Janey pulled the tablet closer again and tried—again—to load the text into the box she'd just finished creating. It looked really cool, with a border of frolicking puppies and kittens and a background of clouds. But when she hit the enter key, all she got in return was an annoying error message—again.

"Aargh!" she cried. "I want to get it working already so I can start getting cute pet photos!"

A bark drifted in through the window. "Maybe that dog outside wants to be on your blog," Lolli joked. "He's telling you to hurry up!"

Janey hopped off her bed and went to the window. A cute golden retriever was sniffing the bushes along the sidewalk. A familiar figure was holding the dog's leash.

"Hey, it's Adam!" Janey told Lolli. "He's walking one of his dog-sitting clients. Let's go ask him if he knows how to work the blog software."

"Adam?" Lolli sounded dubious. "He's not that interested in computers— just dogs."

Janey tucked her tablet under her arm and headed for the door. "Still, he's smart, right?" she said. "Maybe he can figure out what we're doing wrong. Besides, I love that golden retriever he's walking right now—I want to go out and pet him."

Lolli smiled. "In that case, what are we waiting for?"

The big, friendly dog greeted Janey and Lolli happily. So did Adam. But he shook his head as he studied the blog screen.

"Sorry, guys," he said. "I have no clue. Maybe you should ask Zach. He's practically a technology genius."

"Zach? Really?" Now it was Janey's turn to be doubtful. She didn't think Zach was good at anything except being totally obnoxious!

"Uh huh." Adam bent down to untangle the leash from around the golden retriever's leg. "He helped my parents set up a photo-sharing site last year so my relatives can all see pictures of my little sisters and me. And he's always fixing the computer his dad uses for work. I bet a blogging site will be no problem for him."

"It's worth a try," Lolli said. "Zach lives

near here, doesn't he?"

"He's on the next block," Janey said. She frowned at Adam. "Are you sure he's good with computer stuff? What if he wrecks my new tablet?"

"He won't," Adam said. "Trust me, he can get your blog working if anyone can."

Janey sighed. "Fine," she said. "I guess we can go see if he's home. I'd do just about anything to get my blog started!"

4
Going Live

"There he is," Lolli said as the girls turned the corner onto Zach's block.

Janey saw him, too. Zach was in front of his house. He was messing around with his skateboard, trying to get it to jump over a big crack in the sidewalk.

"Hi," Janey said, hurrying up to him. "What are you doing?"

"Learning Chinese," Zach said with a smirk. "What does it look like?"

Janey looked at the house. Loud music was coming out of an open window. "Is someone having a party?"

"Nah, that's just my older brothers." Zach rolled his eyes. "A bunch of their dumb friends came over. They're lucky my dad is the only one home. My mom would never let them play their stupid music so loud."

"Where's your mom?" Lolli asked.

Zach flipped his skateboard up, catching it in one hand. "At work. Her clinic is open on Saturdays."

"Oh." Janey thought it was so cool that Zach's mom was a veterinarian. That was practically her dream job! She didn't say that, though. She figured Zach would probably just make fun of her. "Listen, Adam says you're good at computers...."

She and Lolli told him about all the problems they were having. When Janey held out her tablet, Zach's eyes lit up.

"Cool!" he exclaimed. "I've been dying to get one of these!" Then his face fell. "I probably won't, though. My parents say one computer is enough for the whole family to share."

"We only have one computer, too," Lolli told him.

Zach grinned. "Yeah, but that's because your parents are weirdos," he teased her.

"They are not!" Janey retorted with a frown.

But Lolli just laughed. "It's okay. Mom and Dad call themselves weirdos all the time. So Zach, do you think you can help us with the blog?"

"Duh, that's easy." Zach sat down on his skateboard with the tablet on his lap. His fingers flew over the keypad.

"What are you doing?" Janey couldn't help being a little nervous. What if Zach broke her new tablet? Then she'd have to wait until she got it fixed to start her blog.

Zach didn't answer for a second. Finally he looked up and grinned. "There," he said, showing Janey the screen. "Is that all you needed me to do?"

Janey gasped. The blog looked perfect! The text was exactly where it was supposed to be. Zach had cropped and resized the photos of cats and dogs Janey had pasted onto the page, too. She hadn't asked him to do that, but the photos looked better, so she didn't complain.

"Awesome!" she said. "Thanks, you really…"

She cut herself off with a gasp. Something was happening on the screen. As Janey stared in horror, the edges of her blog page seemed to peel back. Then a cartoon dinosaur leaped into view and started chomping on the text box!

"Hey!" she cried while Zach started laughing so hard he almost fell off his skateboard. "You did that on purpose, didn't you?"

"No, it must be a virus or something." Zach was laughing so hard he could barely get the words out. "You should see your face, Janey!"

Lolli giggled. "That's pretty funny, Zach," she said. "How'd you do it?"

"I could tell you, but you wouldn't understand." Zach grinned. "Cool, right?"

"No." Janey was still frowning. "Fix it!"

"Okay, okay." Zach rolled his eyes. "Next birthday, make sure you ask for a sense of humor, okay?"

Lolli smiled at Janey. "Come on, it was a little bit funny, right?" Lolli said in her soothing way. "Besides, I'm sure Zach is going to fix it right now. Right, Zach?"

"Right." Zach was already bent over the tablet again.

Janey was tempted to grab it away from him. But she decided to give Zach one more chance.

And ten minutes later, she was glad. Zach got rid of the dinosaur and adjusted a few other things. Now the blog looked perfect!

"There," Zach said, pressing a key on-screen. "You're live. Kids should be able to see the blog now."

"Thanks, Zach!" Janey took her tablet back and smiled at the screen. "I can't wait for the cute pet pictures to start coming in!"

⌒

"How's the blog going, sweetheart?" Janey's father asked the next day as Janey helped him clear the lunch dishes.

"Fab." Janey dropped a handful of silverware into the dishwasher. Then she hurried back to the table and picked up her tablet. "People are already posting tons of awesome pictures! This one's my favorite so far."

She scrolled down and showed him a

photo of an adorable black-and-white cat leaping at a butterfly. Her father chuckled.

"Very cute," he agreed. He checked his watch. "Ready to head over to Lolli's? I want to be back here before the game starts on TV."

Janey nodded. She'd made plans to spend Sunday afternoon over at Lolli's house so they could write the next blog entry together. Janey was planning to post every few days with her thoughts about animals and anything else she could think of to write about. She was also going to choose her favorite photos in several categories— cutest pet, funniest pose, best action shot, and other stuff like that. She figured that would encourage people to keep sending photos.

It took about ten minutes to drive to Lolli's farm on the edge of town. Soon the Whitfields' car was bumping and jangling up the Simpsons' long gravel driveway. There was an orchard on one side, and a pasture on the other with two goats and a sheep in it. Usually Janey liked to stop and say hello to the animals, but today she just waved at them as the car passed.

"Have fun," her father said as he stopped in front of the Simpsons' two-story, pointy-roofed farmhouse. The wooden porch sagged a little, and a small flock of chickens was pecking at the dandelions growing on the front lawn. It was very different from the Whitfields' tidy suburban home. But Janey thought the farmhouse was beautiful. She and Lolli had helped

Mrs. Simpson paint the shutters a gorgeous shade of sky blue. And everywhere she looked, something was blooming.

As Janey climbed out of the car, the front door opened. Roscoe bounded out, barking happily.

"Hey, buddy!" Janey greeted Roscoe as he almost crashed into her.

Lolli was right behind Roscoe. She waved to Janey's father as he drove away. Then she grabbed Roscoe by the collar and pulled him away from Janey.

"Leave her alone, Roscoe," she said. "You'll make her drop her tablet!"

"Don't worry, I'm holding on tight," Janey said with a laugh. "Ready to see more cute pictures?"

Just then the tablet let out a ping. "Ooh!" Lolli said. "Does that mean someone else just posted a photo?"

"Uh huh. We should try to guess what kind of animal it will be this time," Janey said, holding her hand over the screen. "I'll guess that it's a fluffy long-haired cat."

"I guess it's, um, a cute potbelly pig," Lolli said with a giggle.

"And the answer is…" Janey moved her hand and looked.

Then she gasped. The picture wasn't of a cat, or of a potbelly pig, either. It wasn't anything cute at all.

It showed a cowering, matted, skinny little gray dog chained in a bare yard.

5

Search and Rescue

"Oh, it's horrible!" Janey blurted out. She wished she hadn't seen the photo at all. The dog looked miserable. He had floppy ears and big, brown eyes. Other than that, he was so dirty and dusty that Janey couldn't even guess what kind of dog he was.

Lolli's eyes filled with tears. "Who would treat a dog like that?" she cried. "We have to do something!"

"What can we do?" Janey rubbed Roscoe's head.

"Let's go ask Mom and Dad." Lolli grabbed the tablet and hurried into the house.

The inside of the farmhouse smelled like scented candles, coffee, and Roscoe. Lolli's parents were sitting at the big wooden kitchen table drinking coffee and reading the Sunday newspaper.

When Lolli showed them the picture,

her mother looked concerned. "Oh, the poor thing," she said.

Lolli's father ran a hand through his curly hair. "Where did this photo come from, girls?" he asked.

"I'm not sure." Janey shrugged. "Whoever sent it didn't put her name on it."

"What can we do to help that dog?" Lolli asked her parents.

Mr. and Mrs. Simpson glanced at each other. "That's our girl," Mr. Simpson said. "The only thing necessary for evil to triumph is for good men to do nothing.'"

"Huh?" Janey blinked. Was Lolli's dad going crazy, or did he think she and Lolli were men?

"It's a famous quotation," Mrs. Simpson explained with a smile. "It means we're very proud of you two for wanting to get involved."

Lolli's father nodded. "Why don't you forward that photo to the animal shelter?" he suggested. "The people there will know how to get the authorities on the case."

"Good idea." Janey found the shelter's website. She forwarded the photo of the skinny dog to the email address on the contact page.

"I hope they can help that dog," Lolli said softly, staring at the photo.

Janey glanced at it one more time, then shuddered and clicked it off. She didn't want to look at the poor little dog's sad face any longer.

"Let's look at some nicer pictures now," she said.

But it didn't work. Janey couldn't stop thinking about the sad gray dog for the rest of the day.

⌒

"I can't stand it any longer," Janey told Lolli the next day at recess. "I'm going to ask Ms. Tanaka if I can call the shelter."

"Good idea," Lolli agreed.

Their homeroom teacher, Ms. Tanaka, was the playground monitor that day. Janey was glad it was her and not grumpy old Mr. Wells. Ms. Tanaka was young and wore cool clothes and laughed a lot.

"Oh, wow," Ms. Tanaka said when she heard about the neglected dog. "Go ahead and check in with the shelter. Here—you can use my phone."

"Thanks." Janey took the phone the teacher handed her.

"Third Street Animal Shelter, may I help you?"a familiar-sounding voice answered when Janey called the shelter's number.

"Kitty? Is that you?" Janey said. She told the shelter worker who she was and why she was calling.

"Oh, I'm so glad you checked in, Janey," Kitty replied. "Do you know anything else about the dog in that photo?"

"No." Janey clutched the phone tighter. "That's why I sent it to you guys. That dog needs help!"

"Oh, yes, we agree." Kitty sounded apologetic. "We forwarded the photo to the town's animal control officer. But she can't take action since nobody knows where the dog is located. If you can find out more, please call us back, okay?"

"Um, okay." Janey wasn't sure how Kitty expected her to find out more. She was just a kid!

She hung up the phone and gave it back to Ms. Tanaka. The teacher was listening to a third grader complain about a boy teasing her, so she just nodded and smiled.

Then Janey went back over to Lolli and told her what Kitty had said. "Now what?" Janey finished. "We have to figure out how to help that dog!"

"Yes, definitely," Lolli agreed, looking worried. She glanced toward the playing field, where several kids were kicking a soccer ball around. "Adam's over there. Let's see if he has any ideas."

They called Adam over, showed him the dog's picture, and told him what was going on. "Wow," he said with a frown. "That's messed up. How can anyone keep a dog that way?"

"Have you ever seen this dog?" Janey asked him. "You know—while you're out walking dogs and stuff?"

"No way." Adam shook his head. "I'd definitely remember!"

Janey bit her lip. Adam walked dogs all over town. "What if that dog isn't even around here?" she wondered. "It could come from a town miles away. Then we'll never find—hey, watch it!"

Zach was zooming straight toward her on his skateboard. He stopped just in time to avoid crashing into her.

"Hey." He grinned. "I didn't scare you, did I? So how's the blog business?"

Janey didn't answer. She wished Zach

would go away. But Lolli and Adam started telling him about the skinny dog.

"…but we don't know where the dog is, so they can't help him," Lolli finished.

"No problem." Zach grabbed Janey's tablet out of her hand. "I can find out who sent the photo. Then all you have to do is track him down and ask where he saw the dog."

"You can?" Adam brightened. "How?"

Zach was already typing on the keypad. "You need to have a verified name and address to post on the blog," he mumbled as he worked. "It's part of the kid-safe software." He hit one more key. "Here you go—this is who sent that picture."

"Vanessa Chaudhry," Lolli read aloud. Her eyes widened. "Hey, she goes to this school!"

Janey knew Vanessa, too. She was the best singer in the fifth grade—she always had solos in the school concerts. "The fifth graders should be coming out for recess while we're on our way in," Janey said. "Let's try to talk to her then."

Vanessa looked startled when Janey and the others surrounded her a few minutes later. At first she tried to deny she'd taken the picture. But when Janey told her that the animal shelter couldn't help the dog without more information, Vanessa bit her lip.

"Oh! I thought posting the picture

would be enough," she said. "I really want someone to rescue that poor dog."

"Then tell us where he is!" Janey urged. "We won't tell anyone you told us."

"Okay." Vanessa described where she'd seen the dog. It was a rural area on the opposite side of town from Lolli's farm. "I really hope you can help him," Vanessa added as Ms. Tanaka headed over to shoo Janey and her classmates inside. "No dog should have to live like that."

6
Truman is Safe!

"They got him!" Janey cried, bursting out of the school's main office.

It was the next afternoon. Mr. Wells had dismissed the class a few minutes earlier. Janey had run straight to the office so she could use the phone there to call the shelter.

"Hip hip hooray!" Lolli cheered, jumping up and down. "What did Kitty say?"

"The animal control officer went out yesterday and talked to the dog's owners," Janey said. She and Lolli wandered down the hall toward the school exit. "They agreed to give the dog to the shelter. He's there now!"

"We should go see him!" Lolli grabbed Janey's arm. "Let's call home and see if our parents will let us walk over to the shelter."

They turned around and rushed back to the office. They got there at the same time as Ms. Tanaka.

"Everything okay, girls?" the teacher asked.

"Yes," Janey replied. "We just need to use the phone."

Ms. Tanaka nodded and held the door open for them. Then the teacher went to check her office mail cubby as the girls headed toward the desk to ask the secretary for permission to use the phone.

"You can call first," Janey told Lolli.

Lolli's father gave permission right away.

But when Janey called home, her mother sounded reluctant. "Maybe you should come home first," she said. "I can drive you and Lolli to the shelter."

"Please, Mom. We don't want to wait that long. Besides, the shelter is only a few blocks from school," Janey said. "Lolli's parents already said yes."

"That's right, Mrs. Whitfield," Lolli said, leaning over Janey's shoulder to talk into the phone. "We'll be careful, we promise!"

"Did I hear you girls say you're going to the Third Street Shelter?" Ms. Tanaka asked, walking over.

"Maybe," Janey said. "If I can talk my mom into saying yes."

Ms. Tanaka smiled. "If it helps, you can tell her I'll walk there with you," she offered. "I was thinking about heading over there myself."

Her offer did help. Janey's mother finally said it was okay. Soon Janey, Lolli, and Ms. Tanaka were walking down the sidewalk toward Third Street.

"Why are you going to the shelter?" Lolli asked her teacher.

Ms. Tanaka chuckled. "Actually, you guys inspired me. I just moved to a new apartment last month, and this one allows pets. I've been thinking about getting a dog, and hearing you talk about the shelter made me decide it's time to start looking for the perfect best friend."

"That's awesome!" For a second, Jane was envious. It seemed everyone could have a pet except her! Then she had a great idea. "I know—you should adopt the dog we saved!"

"Hmm. I like the idea of rescuing a dog that really needs me." Ms. Tanaka sounded interested. "What does he look like?"

Janey showed her the picture from her blog. "He looks kind of bad here," she said. "But I bet all he needs is a good brushing and some food and he'll be super cute!"

"Oh, he's cute—but awfully small. I was thinking about a bigger dog." Ms. Tanaka smiled. "See, I had horses growing up, so I'm used to big pets. A really huge dog is the next best thing to a horse!"

Lolli laughed, while Janey smiled weakly. "Are you sure you don't want him?" she asked.

"Sorry." Ms. Tanaka patted her arm. "But don't worry—your dog is adorable. I'm sure he'll find a home fast."

When they reached the shelter, Ms. Tanaka said good-bye and headed into the dog room. Meanwhile, Kitty rushed over to greet the girls.

"I'm so glad you came!" she said. "Stay right here, and I'll go get Truman so he can thank you in person!"

"Truman?" Janey echoed.

"That's the dog you saved. He's a real sweetie." Kitty smiled. "Be right back."

Moments later she returned with a dog on a leash. Janey barely recognized him from his picture! Someone had given him a bath, brushed the tangles out of his silky fur, and trimmed the hair on his ears and paws.

Janey had memorized every breed from her dog books, and she thought Truman looked as if he might be a cross between a schnauzer and a shih tzu. Whatever he was, he was one of the cutest dogs she'd ever seen!

"Oh, you're so adorable!" she cried, reaching for him.

Truman ducked away from her touch, but his short tail was wagging and his ears were pricked with curiosity. "You'll have to take it easy and be patient with him," Kitty advised. "He's still a little shy. But he's very sweet once he trusts you. Come on—let's hang out in the Meet and Greet room so you can all get to know each other."

They all went into the small room. Truman sniffed everything carefully, then flopped down on one of the beanbag chairs. Meanwhile Kitty told the girls what the animal officer had found out.

"Truman belonged to an elderly man who adored him," she said. "Then the owner died, and Truman went to live with the man's relatives. But one of the kids in the house was allergic."

"Just like Janey's dad," Lolli said.

Janey nodded. "The family stuck him outside and kind of forgot about him, I guess. One of the other kids was supposed to feed him and give him water but he didn't always remember."

Janey clenched her fists. "How could anyone be so horrible?" she exclaimed. "Especially with sweet dog like Truman!"

"Try not to think about it," Lolli advised. "He's safe now, and I'm sure somebody great will adopt him."

"I wish I could adopt him," Janey said.

Lolli gave her a sympathetic smile. "Try not to think about that, either."

Janey tried. For the next hour, she and Lolli stayed with Truman. He was shy at first, but eventually he seemed to decide the girls were okay. After that, they could hardly get him to stop playing!

Janey was disappointed when her mother arrived to pick them up. "We'll come visit you again soon, Truman," she promised the little dog.

"Right," Lolli agreed. "Unless someone adopts you before that!"

"I'm sure it won't take long." Janey smiled and rubbed Truman's silky ears. She giggled as the little dog licked her from her chin to her forehead. "Who could resist a face—or a tongue—like that?"

7
Still Waiting

"Did you call the shelter last night?" Lolli asked when Janey walked into school on Thursday morning.

Janey nodded and sighed. "He's still there."

"I don't get it." Lolli leaned against the wall of cubbies, watching as Janey put her stuff away. "Truman is such a great dog! Why doesn't anyone want to take him home?"

"I have no idea." Janey was about to put her tablet in the cubby with the rest of her things. Then she stopped and stared at it. "But I just thought of something. My blog was what saved Truman, right? Maybe it can also help him find the perfect home!"

"What do you mean?" Lolli asked.

Janey was already logging onto the internet. "I'm going to post an update about Truman. Lots of people saw the picture of him on my blog."

"That's true," Lolli agreed. "You got tons of comments about how horrible he looked."

"So now I'll tell everyone he's safe and looking for a home." Janey typed quickly, describing how the animal officer had saved Truman. She added that the little dog was at the shelter waiting for an adopter to come and take him home.

Lolli watched over her shoulder. "Don't forget to mention how cute he looks now that he's healthy and clean," she suggested.

Janey nodded. She wished she'd taken pictures of Truman at the shelter. Maybe she could get some later. But her words would have to do for now.

"There!" she said, hitting the key to post the blurb. "That should do the trick."

But when Janey called the shelter again on Saturday, Kitty told her that Truman was still there.

"Your ad *did* work, though," Kitty added. "Sort of, anyway. Three different people came in looking for Truman because they'd seen him on your blog."

"Really? Then why is he still there?" Janey asked.

"They all decided he wasn't quite right for them," Kitty said. "They all chose different dogs instead."

"Oh." Janey sighed. "Oh, well, lots of people come to get new pets on the weekend, right? Someone will probably take him home soon. Lolli and I will be right over—we want to see him again before he finds his new owners."

Soon the two friends were at the shelter playing with Truman. A family was in the Meet and Greet room getting to know a few of the shelter's cats, so the girls tossed a rubber bone for Truman in the wide, rubber-paved aisle of the dog room. There were dogs in the runs on either side of the aisle, but Truman paid little attention to them, staying focused on the girls.

"Good boy!" Janey exclaimed when Truman pounced on the bone and then brought it back to her. "You already know how to fetch!"

"He's super smart." said Lolli as she ruffled Truman's ears. "Aren't you, boy?"

Just then the door to the dog room opened. Kitty walked in, followed by a nicely dressed man and woman and a five-year-old boy.

"Excuse me, girls," Kitty said. "This lovely family has come to see Truman."

"That's right." The mother had a nice smile. "Are you Janey? We saw what you wrote about Truman on your blog, and we just had to meet him!"

Her husband nodded. "We were planning to get a dog this weekend anyway, and we think Truman might be perfect. Is that him?"

"Yes, this is Truman." Janey saw that Truman was backing away from the man. "Um, he's a little shy with new people."

"He's cute! Here, Truman!" The little boy rushed toward Truman, who quickly sidled out of reach.

"Slow down, son," his father called. "You don't want to startle him."

He strode over and grabbed Truman before the little dog could get away. "Careful," Kitty warned. "He's still getting used to things here, and…"

"Easy, fella! We just want to pet you, that's all." The man hugged Truman to his chest. Truman struggled against his grip, looking anxious.

"Why don't you let me hold him for you?" Janey said quickly. "He knows me, so that will help him relax."

"Ow!" the man said as Truman scrabbled against his chest, looking frantic now. "Oh, no! He just put a hole in my new shirt!"

He set Truman down and peered down at his golf shirt. Truman darted behind Janey and pressed himself against her legs. She could feel him trembling.

"It's just a shirt, Steve," the man's wife said, rolling her eyes. "But perhaps Truman isn't quite right for us after all. We don't want a dog we need to tiptoe around."

The little boy already seemed to have forgotten all about Truman. He was over by one of the runs, reaching in to pet a friendly hound mix.

"I want this one!" he cried. "Look—he likes me!"

"Can we meet that one?" the man asked
Kitty. "He seems like a good family dog."

Kitty shot Truman an anxious glance.
"Sure, let's take him over to the Meet and
Greet," she said. "I think the cats are out of
there now."

As soon as the family had disappeared,

along with Kitty and the hound mix, Truman came out of hiding. He grabbed the rubber bone and dropped it at Lolli's feet, wagging his tail.

Janey sighed. "Oh, Truman," she said, kneeling down to give the dog a hug. "You're such a sweetie pie. Why can't anyone but us see that?"

8

A Plan for Truman

A little while later, Kitty returned. "Well, at least Chance found a new home," she said, gesturing at the empty run where the hound mix had been. "That family loved him, and it was totally mutual. I think it's a great match." She bent to pat Truman, who was sniffing at her shoe. "I just wish this little guy would find his perfect match."

"Me, too," Janey said. "I can't believe nobody wants him!"

Kitty sighed. "I know. Poor Truman was just a little too shy or a little too untrained for all the people who were interested in him so far."

Just then the door opened again. Zach burst into the dog room, followed by his mother. "Yo, Truman!" Zach exclaimed loudly when he spotted the dog. "Are these girls bothering you, little guy?"

He rushed over to the dog. Janey expected Truman to try to get away, but instead he barked and jumped up on Zach's legs. Zach laughed and rubbed Truman's ears.

"Hey, he's being friendly now," Lolli said.

"Sure he is, he's my buddy." Zach grabbed the rubber bone and tossed it. Truman barked and leaped off to retrieve it.

Dr. Goldman chuckled. "Don't even think about asking again to take him home," she warned Zach. She glanced at the girls. "Zach was with me when I did Truman's intake checkup and shots the other day. As you can see, the two of them hit it off."

"Is that why you two stopped by?" Kitty asked the vet with a grin. "To adopt Truman?"

"Actually, I stopped by to take that new cat's stitches out. Seeing Truman is a bonus, but I'm afraid we can't take him home. We already have a cat, which is about all I can handle with four boys, a busy vet practice, and an absent-minded husband who gets so caught up in his work that he's not likely to remember to walk a dog unless it's actually piddling on his foot." She smiled at Janey and Lolli. "Is one of you thinking about adopting Truman?"

"Our parents won't let us take him home, either," Janey said. "And nobody else seems interested, even though he's so fab!"

"Poor Truman." Lolli patted Truman as he trotted past with the rubber bone. "He just needs someone who understands him."

"Maybe." Dr. Goldman pushed Truman down gently as he dropped the bone, barked, and jumped up on her legs. "But he could also use a little training and socializing to make him more adoptable."

"What do you mean?" Janey asked.

"He's a nice dog," the vet said. "But some adopters might not be able to see the diamond in the rough the way we can." She smiled at Janey and Lolli. "If you girls want to help him find a home, maybe you can work with him a little. Teach him a few basic commands, and get him more used to being around people."

"We can do that!" Janey felt a surge of hope. "Right, Lolli?"

"Definitely!" Lolli agreed.

"Yeah," Zach put in. "I can help if you want."

"Thanks, but that's okay," Janey told him. "We've got it covered. Come on Lolli, let's start right now!"

Kitty smiled apologetically. "Actually, you'll need to get your parents to sign our volunteer form before you can do any real training or take him for walks outside," she said. "Sorry. I probably shouldn't even have let you spend all this time with him before doing that."

Janey frowned, feeling impatient. But Lolli nodded. "We can do that," she said. "We were planning to ask about volunteering here anyway, and both our parents already said it was okay, so I'm sure they'll sign. I'll call my mom to come get us, and then we'll be back as soon as we have the forms filled out and signed."

"You girls are lucky that this shelter lets kids volunteer," Dr. Goldman told them with a smile. "I would've loved to get involved like that as a kid, but the shelter in the town where I grew up only allows people over eighteen to handle the animals."

"Not here," Kitty said cheerfully. "We've found that younger kids are great with the animals! Come on, girls—let's get you those forms."

Over the next week, Janey went to the shelter as often as she could to work with Truman. Lolli usually came, too. Even Adam took some time out of his busy dog-walking schedule to show the girls some training techniques. Janey knew that Adam had

worked with lots of dogs, but she was impressed by how quickly he taught Truman the commands for sit, stay, come, and heel.

Truman seemed to enjoy all the attention. After a few days, Kitty reported that he was already acting friendlier with people—even ones he didn't know.

"He's a fast learner," she said as she watched Truman follow Janey around the lobby on Friday afternoon, staying right at her heel. "And you kids are great teachers! I bet he'll find his new family before long."

"I sure hope you're right. Sit, Truman!" Janey beamed as the little dog lowered his haunches to the floor. "Good boy!"

9

A Perfect Pair?

"I wish we didn't have to take him back to the shelter," Janey said as she turned the corner onto Third Street. It was early Sunday afternoon and she, Lolli, and Adam had just helped Kitty take Truman to the town park for a walk. The little dog had behaved perfectly, walking politely on his leash, letting several strangers pet him, and even standing quietly while a woman pushed a screaming baby past in a stroller.

"We shouldn't keep him out too long, though," Adam pointed out. "Lots of people come to the shelter on Sundays."

"That's right." Kitty gave a gentle tug on Truman's leash as he stopped to sniff at a leaf on the sidewalk. "We don't want him to miss being seen by his perfect adopter."

"True." Janey felt a pang of sadness. Even though they were all working hard to make Truman more adoptable, she hated to think that she might not get to see him anymore once he went to his new home.

When they entered the lobby, Truman barked and leaped forward. Zach and his mother were by the desk with one of Kitty's co-workers. Zach was balanced on one foot on his skateboard while Dr. Goldman examined a fat white cat's paw.

"Hi, Truman!" Zach exclaimed, hurrying forward to greet the little dog. "What's up?"

"We just went for a walk." Janey took Truman's leash from Kitty, and pulled him in closer. "Truman did fab. We're still working on his training, you know."

"Yeah, I heard." Zach rubbed Truman's head. "I bet someone will adopt him soon."

Janey nodded, stepping out of the way as the other shelter worker walked past carrying the white cat. "I'm thinking of posting again on my blog about how great Truman is doing," Janey said. "I bet that will get more people to come see him."

The bell over the shelter door tinkled as someone entered. Janey was surprised to see that it was Ms. Tanaka.

"Hi, kids!" The teacher seemed surprised to see them, too. She smiled. "You sure spend a lot of time here, don't you?"

"What can I say?" Zach shrugged and hooked a thumb toward his mother. "My mom drags me here all the time."

"I think she was talking to us," Janey informed him. "Hi, Ms. T. Didn't you already pick out a dog last weekend?" She'd been so busy thinking about Truman that she'd almost forgotten about her teacher's quest for a pet. But now she was curious.

"Not yet." The teacher shrugged. "There are lots of great dogs here, but I couldn't decide on one, so I decided to wait and think about it."

"So you came back for another look?" Kitty asked cheerfully. "I can help you as soon as I finish showing Dr. Goldman her next patient, okay?"

"No hurry, thanks." Ms. Tanaka smiled as Kitty and Dr. Goldman headed off into the dog room. Then she patted Truman as he trotted over to say hi. "Who have we here?"

"This is Truman—the dog we showed you before," Lolli told her.

Ms. Tanaka looked surprised. "Really? Wow, I didn't recognize him! He looks totally different from that poor, scraggly dog in the picture." She rubbed his ears, smiling as he slurped her hands and then rolled onto his back, begging for a belly rub. "Too bad he's not a little bigger."

Janey shot Lolli and Adam a look. Ms. Tanaka really seemed to like Truman—and he seemed to like her, too. Maybe they'd given up on her too easily!

"He might not be that big, but he's got a huge personality," Janey told Ms. Tanaka. "He's just about fully trained, too—watch!" She snapped her fingers to get Truman's attention. "Truman, heel!"

She quickly put Truman through his paces, demonstrating all the commands he could do. Truman got a little distracted when a shelter worker led a tiny, fluffy dog past, heading for the Meet and Greet room. But otherwise he was practically perfect!

When the demonstration was finished, Ms. Tanaka was smiling. "Very impressive,

Janey," she said. "Truman is cute. He'll make someone a fantastic friend. I'm just not sure he's quite what I'm looking for."

"Are you sure?" Janey's heart sank. What more could they do to convince her?

Zach stepped forward. "Can I take him for a sec?" he asked, reaching for Truman's leash.

Janey almost didn't hand him the leash. This was no time for Zach to start goofing around! She was sure if she could just figure out how to change Ms. Tanaka's mind some-how...

But she didn't resist as Zach took the leash. "Okay, Janey already showed you the boring stuff," he told Ms. Tanaka with a grin. "Now watch this!"

"What's he doing?" Lolli murmured, leaning toward Janey.

Janey shrugged. She watched as Zach kneeled down in front of Truman.

"Okay, Truman," he said, lifting his hand. "High five!"

Truman barked. Then he jumped up, smacking his front paws onto Zach's palm.

"Oh, that's cute!" Ms. Tanaka exclaimed with a laugh. "Did you really teach him to high-five, Zach?"

"That's nothing," Zach said. "Check this out." He grabbed his skateboard and set it in front of Truman.

"Who taught Truman to high-five?" Lolli sounded confused.

Janey knew how she felt. She watched as

Truman jumped onto Zach's skateboard and then used his hind leg to push off, barking happily as he rode the skateboard halfway across the lobby.

This time Ms. Tanaka laughed out loud and clapped. "That's so cool!" she exclaimed. "Did you teach him that, Zach? Very impressive!"

Zach grinned and bowed. "Thank you, it was nothing," he said. "I've been coming by and teaching Truman a few tricks while Mom's here working."

Janey frowned, not sure whether to be impressed or annoyed. Then she noticed that Ms. Tanaka was kneeling down and patting Truman, whose whole body seemed to be wagging as he enjoyed the attention.

"Truman is great, isn't he?" Janey told her teacher. And then she had an idea. "He's kind of like a big dog in a little dog's body, right?"

"Yeah," Adam put in. "I've worked with a lot of dogs, and Truman is one of the coolest. Seriously."

Lolli nodded vigorously. "And I think he really likes you, Ms. Tanaka."

The teacher laughed, holding up her hands. "Okay, enough with the hard sell, gang," she said. "You don't need to convince me—Truman already did that."

"What? Really?" Janey wasn't sure she'd heard her right.

"Really." Ms. Tanaka gave Truman one last pat, then straightened up. "Actually, I've been thinking my apartment might be kind of small for a big dog. And now I'm totally convinced. Besides, a bigger dog couldn't ride a skateboard like that, right?" She winked. "Anyway, when Kitty comes back I think I'll talk to her about taking Truman home with me so I can see what other fun tricks I can teach him. What do you say, Truman?"

Truman barked and danced around her legs. Janey let out a whoop of joy. Talk about a happy ending!

10

Happy Endings... and Beginnings

"Leave that alone, Roscoe." Lolli tugged on her dog's leash as he stopped to sniff at a pinecone on the sidewalk. "Come on, we're almost there."

Janey stopped to let them catch up. It was Tuesday afternoon, and she and Lolli had decided to take Roscoe to the town park.

"Hey, look who's here!" Lolli said as they entered the park. "It's Ms. Tanaka and Truman!"

Janey looked where she was pointing. Their teacher was halfway across the park in a grassy area shaded by some huge old oak trees. Truman was there, too, chasing a ball his new owner was throwing for him.

"I still can't believe how great everything turned out." Lolli smiled as she watched the pair playing. "It's like it was meant to be!"

"I know, right?" Janey nodded. "Ms. Tanaka told me she can't imagine her life without Truman. Isn't that fab?"

"Totally fab," Lolli agreed. "Should we go over and say hi?"

Before she could answer, Janey heard a flurry of barking from the opposite direction. Turning to look, she saw Adam coming with one of his doggy clients, a pretty collie mix. Zach was with him, pushing himself along on his skateboard.

Roscoe's whole hind end wagged along with his tail as he greeted the other dog. The collie mix barked, then came forward to sniff Roscoe's nose.

"It's okay," Adam told Lolli. "This guy is friendly with other dogs. And I know Roscoe is, too."

Zach was peering across the park. "Hey, there's Ms. T. and Truman," he said.

"Yeah, we just saw them, too," Janey said. "We were about to go say hi. Want to come?"

"In a minute." Adam glanced at Zach. "Actually, it's good that we ran into you. Zach has an idea he wants to tell you about."

"An idea?" Janey looked at Zach. "What kind of idea?"

Zach flipped his skateboard and tried to jump back on, but he missed and staggered off a few steps. "It's an idea about breaking my leg," he joked. "I'm working on it now."

Adam smiled. "No, seriously, tell them, dude," he said. "I think they'll like it."

"What is it, Zach?" Lolli asked.

Zach patted Roscoe as the big dog came over to sniff at him. "It's no big deal," he said. "Just something I was thinking about, you know? After what happened with Truman, and everything…."

Janey sighed. "Just spit it out already," she said. "We don't have all day."

Zach smirked. "Why not? Do you have an appointment with the President of the United States or something?"

"Just tell them," Adam said.

Zach shrugged. "Okay. See, we did such a great job getting Truman the perfect home, right? All of us helped."

"That's true," Lolli agreed.

Janey nodded. She had to admit that Zach's tricks had probably won over Ms. Tanaka just as much as the training she, Lolli, and Adam had done.

"So." Zach paused, glancing over toward Truman again. "I was thinking we should, you know, do more of that."

"You mean we should volunteer at the shelter?" Janey said. "We're already planning to."

"Not just that," Adam said. "He thinks we should form, like, a club or something."

"Yeah." Zach sounded excited now. "I was thinking we could call it the Pet Rescue Club! I bet there are lots of other animals right here in our town who need our help. We could use your blog to find them, and then to help find them homes— just like with Truman. And, well, like I said the four of us make a pretty good team…"

Lolli smiled. "What a super idea!" she exclaimed.

But, Janey hesitated. She wasn't so sure. For one thing, Zach was pretty annoying sometimes. Did she really want to be in a club with him?

"What do you think, Janey?" Adam asked.

"I don't know," Janey said slowly. "My blog is supposed to be for sharing cute pet photos, not for stuff like that. Seeing that first picture of Truman pop up was really upsetting."

"I know, but it could be for both things, couldn't it?" Lolli said, stroking the collie mix's sleek head. "We'll be able to help other dogs like Truman. And cats and other animals, too, of course."

"Isn't that worth being upset a little bit?" Adam added.

Zach didn't say anything. He was watching Janey carefully, not cracking jokes or messing with his skateboard for once. Janey stared back at him. Would he really take something like this seriously?

She wasn't sure, but she realized something else. It didn't matter. She took helping animals seriously. So did Lolli and Adam, and probably Zach. Working together, she was sure they could make it work.

"I guess you're right," she said with a cautious smile. "Helping Truman made it all worthwhile. And my blog has been getting tons of hits. Everyone loved hearing about Truman's happy ending. It really is the perfect way to reach animals in need."

"Cool!" Zach exclaimed with a grin. "So we're going to do this?"

He raised his hand. Lolli high-fived him. Adam switched the leash he was holding to his other hand and did the same. Then Janey stepped forward and high-fived Zach, too. At least she tried to—at the last second, he pulled his hand away.

"Psych!" he cried with a grin.

Janey frowned. "Very funny."

"Sorry." Zach grabbed her hand and

high-fived it. "So it's official—we're the Pet Rescue Club?"

"Yeah." Janey's mind was already filling with ideas for how to make the club work. It was going to be great! She couldn't believe she hadn't thought of it herself. "It's official. I can't wait to get started!"

Kids Getting Involved

Are you a kid who loves animals and wants to help them? Then get involved! Some shelters allow kids to volunteer, like the one in Janey's town. Others only accept adult volunteers for safety reasons. But even if the shelter in your town is the second kind, there are lots of ways to help needy animals. Here are a few ideas:

1. **Organize** a fund-raiser for your local shelter or rescue.

2. **Donate** food or toys for the shelter pets.

3. **Publicize** your local shelter on your blog, or just by talking to your friends.

4. **Read** your shelter's website and other animal welfare sites to keep up on current needs and issues, and to watch for other ways to help.

5. **Set an example** for all pet owners by always treating your own pet well!

For more ideas, check out:

www.aspca.org/parents/term/
how-your-kids-can-help-shelter-pets

Meet the Real Truman!

A little gray dog named Harry Truman was surrendered to a shelter in Tennessee in 2010. He was skinny and had matted fur. He was sent to a shelter in upstate New York, where he met his future owner. She considered herself a "big dog" person, but Harry Truman convinced her that even little dogs have big hearts!

Look for
the next book in the
**PET RESCUE
CLUB** series!

**Book #2—
No Time for Hallie**

Zach's neighbors have a new baby and now they don't have the time or attention for their cat, Hall Cat. Now they are thinking of bringing Hall Cat to the animal shelter! The kids in the Pet Rescue Club know that an older cat might have trouble getting adopted. Can they convince the family to give their kitty another chance—or perhaps find someone who truly appreciates all that an older cat has to offer? It won't be easy, especially since Janey is busy helping a friend locate a lost canary and Lolli is worried about a sad classmate....